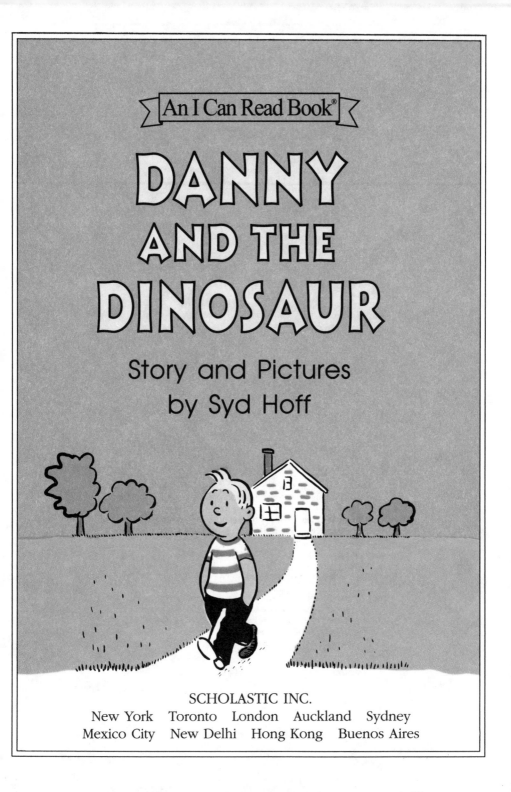

An I Can Read Book®

DANNY AND THE DINOSAUR

Story and Pictures
by Syd Hoff

SCHOLASTIC INC.
New York   Toronto   London   Auckland   Sydney
Mexico City   New Delhi   Hong Kong   Buenos Aires

I Can Read Book® is a registered trademark of HarperCollins Publishers Inc. All Rights Reserved.

Copyright © 1958 by Syd Hoff. Copyright © renewed 1986 by Syd Hoff.
All rights reserved. Published by Scholastic Inc., 557 Broadway,
New York, NY 10012, by arrangement with HarperCollins Publishers.
SCHOLASTIC and associated logos are trademarks
and/or registered trademarks of Scholastic Inc.

ISBN 0-439-45275-9

12 11 10 9 8 7 6 5 4 3 2 1   2 3 4 5 6 7/0

Printed in the U.S.A.

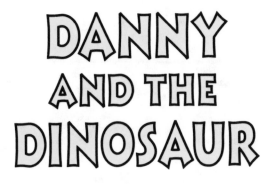

One day Danny went

to the museum.

He wanted to see what was inside.

5

He saw Indians.

He saw bears.

He saw Eskimos.

He saw guns.

He saw swords.

And he saw . . .

DINOSAURS!

8

Danny loved dinosaurs.

He wished he had one.

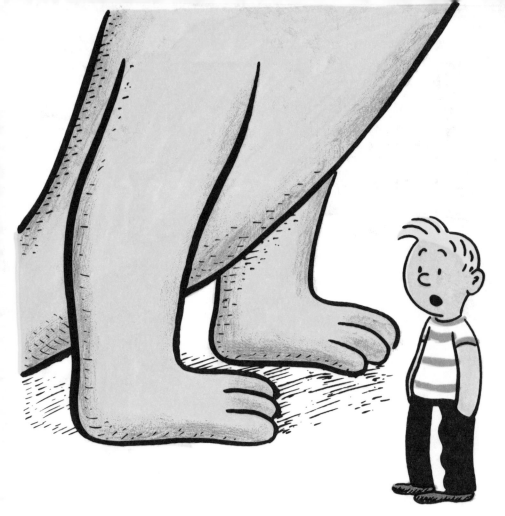

"I'm sorry they are not real,"

said Danny.

"It would be nice

to play with a dinosaur."

10

"And I think it would be nice

to play with you,"

said a voice.

"Can you?" said Danny.

"Yes," said the dinosaur.

"Oh, good," said Danny.

"What can we do?"

"I can take you for a ride,"

said the dinosaur.

He put his head down

so Danny could

get on him.

13

"Let's go!" said Danny.

A policeman stared at them.

He had never seen a dinosaur stop

for a red light.

15

The dinosaur was so tall Danny had
to hold up the ropes for him.

16

"Look out!" said Danny.

17

"Bow wow!" said a dog.

"He thinks you are a car," said Danny.

"Go away, dog. We are not a car."

18

"I can make a noise like a car,"

said the dinosaur.

"Honk! Honk! Honk!"

19

"What big rocks,"

said the dinosaur.

"They are not rocks," said Danny.

"They are buildings."

"I love to climb,"

said the dinosaur.

"Down, boy!" said Danny.

21

The dinosaur had to be very careful
not to knock over houses or stores
with his long tail.

Some people were
waiting for a bus.
They rode on the
dinosaur's tail instead.

"All who want

to cross the street

may walk on my back,"

said the dinosaur.

24

"It's very nice of you to help me
with my bundles," said a lady.

25

Danny and the dinosaur went

all over town and had lots of fun.

"It's good to take

an hour or two off

after a hundred million years,"

said the dinosaur.

26

They even looked at

the ball game.

"Hit the ball,"

said Danny.

"Hit a home run,"

said the dinosaur.

27

"I wish we had a boat,"

said Danny.

"Who needs a boat?

I can swim,"

said the dinosaur.

"Toot, toot!"

went the boats.

"Toot, toot!" went Danny

and the dinosaur.

29

"Oh, what lovely green grass!"

said the dinosaur.

"I haven't eaten any of that

for a very long time."

"Wait," said Danny.

"See what it says."

30

PLEASE
KEEP
OFF

They both had ice cream instead.

"Let's go to the zoo

and see the animals," said Danny.

32

Everybody came running

to see the dinosaur.

Nobody stayed to see

the lions.

Nobody stayed to see

the elephants.

Nobody stayed to see

the monkeys.

36

And nobody stayed to see

the seals,

giraffes or hippos,

either.

"Please go away

so the animals

will get looked at,"

said the zoo man.

"Let's find my friends,"

said Danny.

"Very well,"

said the dinosaur.

"There they are," said Danny.

"Why, it's Danny

riding on a dinosaur,"

said a child.

"Maybe he'll give us a ride."

"May we have a ride?"

asked the children.

"I'd be delighted,"

said the dinosaur.

"Hold on tight," said Danny.

41

Around and around

the block ran the dinosaur,

faster and faster and faster.

"This is better than

a merry-go-round,"

the children said.

The dinosaur was

out of breath.

"Teach him tricks,"

said the children.

Danny taught the dinosaur

how to shake hands.

"Can you roll over on your back?"

asked the children.

"That's easy,"

said the dinosaur.

"He's smart," said Danny,

patting the dinosaur.

46

"Let's play hide and seek,"

said the children.

"How do you play it?"

said the dinosaur.

"We hide and you try

to find us," said Danny.

47

The dinosaur covered

his eyes.

All the children ran

to hide.

The dinosaur

looked and looked

but he couldn't find the children.

"I give up," he said.

Now it was the dinosaur's turn

to hide.

The children covered their eyes.

The dinosaur hid

behind a house.

The children found him.

He hid behind a sign.

The children

found him.

He hid behind a big gas tank.

The children found him.

They found him again

and again and again.

"I guess there's no place

for me to hide,"

said the dinosaur.

"Let's make believe

we can't find him," Danny said.

"Where can he be?

Where, oh, where is that dinosaur?

Where did he go?

We give up," said the children.

56

"Here I am," said the dinosaur.

"The dinosaur wins,"

said the children.

"We couldn't find him.

He fooled us."

"Hurrah for the dinosaur!"

the children cried.

"Hurray! Hurray!"

59

It got late and

the other children left.

Danny and the dinosaur

were alone.

"Well, goodbye, Danny,"

said the dinosaur.

60

"Can't you come

and stay with me?"

said Danny.

"We could have fun."

"No," said the dinosaur.

"I've had a good time—

the best I've had

in a hundred million years.

But now I must get back

to the museum.

They need me there."

"Oh," said Danny.

"Well, goodbye."

Danny watched

until the long tail

was out of sight.

Then he went home alone.

"Oh, well," thought Danny,

"we don't have room

for a pet that size, anyway.

But we did have

a wonderful day."